Richard Scarry's
Busy Day Storybooks

Father Cat's
Busy Day

It is early morning. Father Cat awakes as the sun comes up.

He looks out of the window. "What a perfect day to put the boat in the water!" he says.

He goes downstairs to the kitchen and prepares breakfast
for the family.

He brings
Mother Cat
a cup
of coffee
in bed.

Father Cat runs outside to his sailboat,
parked beside the garage.

He pulls off the canvas cover, and tries to push the boat
trailer into the driveway. But the trailer won't move.
It has a flat tire. Ungh!

From the garage, Father Cat gets an air pump.

Just then, Mother Cat comes up on her bicycle, holding a shopping list.

"I have to go the the hairdresser," she says. "Could you please do the food shopping for me this morning?"

Then Huckle arrives with his bicycle, Sally with her tricycle, and Lowly with his scooter. Everyone needs air in the tires!

Finally, Father Cat can pump up the trailer tire.

Then he pulls the boat into the driveway.

But it's time
to do the
shopping.

CLONK!

The boat trailer is blocking the
driveway!
Father Cat drives the Cat family
car around the boat, onto the lawn,
crushing a few bushes. Sorry, bushes!
He also knocks over the mailbox.

At the supermarket, Father Cat realizes he has forgotten
Mother Cat's shopping list.
He asks the children to each choose three items from each
shopping aisle. That should please Mother Cat.

After the supermarket,
the car needs some gas.
Father Cat drives into
Scotty's gas station.

While he fills up the car, Scotty takes a look
at the car motor. He pulls out a few pieces and
shows them to Father Cat.
"It's time to replace some parts!" Scotty tells Father Cat.
"Don't worry, it won't take long."

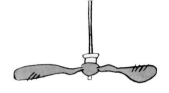

While Father Cat waits for his car to be repaired, he invites
the children across the street for milkshakes.

Meanwhile, back at the Cat family house, the boat trailer has begun to roll down the driveway, and into the street.

Oh, no! Here comes Mr. Frumble in his picklecar!

"Who would sail a boat into the middle of the street!"
Mr. Frumble says.

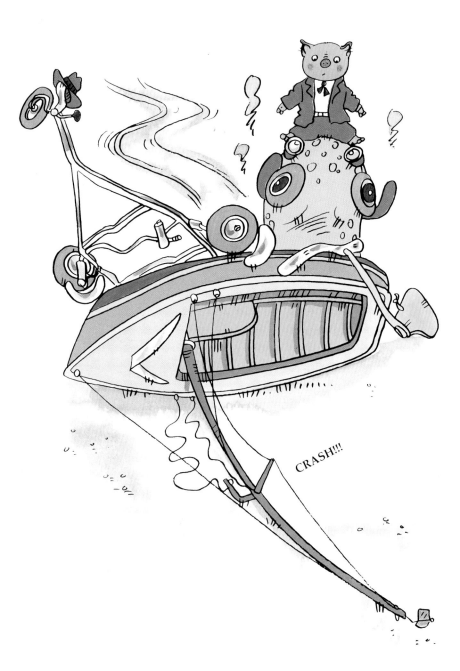

CRASH!!!

Luckily, Mr. Fixit soon arrives on the scene.

With his crane, he removes Father Cat's boat out of harm's way. Then he tows away Mr. Frumble's broken picklecar.

"A good thing that you brought along a trailer, Mr. Frumble!" Mr. Fixit says.

Soon, the Cat family car is ready again.
It looks like the ice-cream somebody
chose at the supermarket has melted.

Now the car needs to go
through the car wash.

At last, they are ready to drive home.
Mother Cat must be wondering
what has happened to them!

But instead, Mother Cat is wondering what has happened to her poor bushes and the mailbox.

Father Cat looks with
surprise at the driveway.

"What has happened to my boat?" he asks.

"I *know* I left the boat in the driveway," Father Cat tells Mother Cat. "It has to be around here somewhere!"

"Well, before you begin to look," says Mother Cat, "perhaps you first want to change out of your pyjamas!"